The Mermaid's adventure

The New Friends

By Diana Molly

Introduction

Daisy and Azalea remember their adventures in Beyondness, which they miss very much. The mermaid sisters decide to have some more adventures, and all they need is a map.

Now, that they have no trouble finding the Pink Sparkle, it seems it will not be difficult to have a good time. But the sisters do not know that everything will go totally different as to what they have planned.

The new girls on the beach have no idea what kind of surprise is in store for them. While all of them enjoy ice-cream, the mermaid sisters use their abilities to save the day for everyone.

Chapter 1

The Great Idea

"Azalea, are you asleep?" Daisy called. It was night, and the two mermaid sisters were already in their shell-beds. Their pretty pink room was dimly lit by a couple of floating seashells that were emitting a faint light. It was silent and peaceful, as their entire underwater city Clover was asleep. Only the gentle songs of the Nightingales of the Ocean were heard from far.

"Not yet, why?" Azalea said.

"I read a new book about Beyondness, today," Daisy said. "I got it from the school library. And it was so interesting. Azalea, do you remember when we were out there in Beyondness a couple of months ago?"

"The time when we rescued the prince? Of course, I do, Daisy!" Azalea exclaimed. "We had the best adventures of our lives. And I miss it, too. I wish we had a chance to see Beyondness again."

"I miss it, too," Daisy said. "Look, I have a very interesting idea."

"Whenever you say that, I have a feeling that a wonderful adventure is waiting for us, Daisy," Azalea said, giggling. "What idea do you have this time?"

"Let's go to Beyondness again," Daisy said in one breath.

"Oh, Daisy, we can't," Azalea said sadly. "School has started. We barely have time to do our lessons! Also, we have extra lessons in Worldology and Biology this term."

"Come on, Azalea," Daisy said to her older sister. "It will not take long! We can go over the surface and swim back. I want to see the sky..."

"I do not know, Daisy," Azalea said. "Well, maybe we can go, but only not now. It is late at night now, and we must not leave the house at night."

"Of course, I know," Daisy said. "We can go in the morning, after breakfast. Tomorrow is not a school day, remember?"

"Yes, it is the millionth birthday of Clover," Azalea agreed. "Well, we can swim to the surface of the ocean in the morning and get back down; if that is all you wish."

"Azalea, you are the best sister in the world!" Daisy exclaimed. "And now, let's sleep – tomorrow we are going to have an adventure!"

"Good night," Azalea said, smiling. "And sweet dreams."

"Good night, the best sister in the world," Daisy said, giggling. She closed her eyes, imagining the morning when they would leave Clover to see the sky and the sun again.

*****

The sisters slept tightly and woke up when it was morning. The shells were emitting bright light, making their room shine brightly. Daisy and Azalea stretched and looked at each other. Both were beautiful – Daisy with long blond hair and blue eyes, and Azalea with long brown hair and bright brown eyes.

"Azalea, you know, I dreamed about Beyondness," Daisy said, smiling. "And it was such a wonderful dream!"

"I believe you," Azalea said, giggling. "All you think about is Beyondness. Of course, your dreams would be about it, too."

"But don't you wish to see it again? Or is it only me who has missed it?" Daisy asked, as she swam out of her pink shell-bed and changed into a pretty golden top.

"Of course, I have missed it, too," Azalea said, stretching and yawning. "We can go there after breakfast."

The two sisters swam into the kitchen, where their mother was making breakfast.

"Good morning, mom, how are you?" Azalea said.

"And what are you making?" Daisy asked, looking at the food on the table.

"Very well, my dear daughters," she said. "I am making Petal and Root salad for breakfast."

"Oh, that is my favorite!" Daisy exclaimed.

"We can help you, mom," Azalea added. "Today it is a day off from school."

Their mother smiled. "Of course, my dear. I will be delighted if you help me."

"It is such a beautiful day today," Daisy said, taking the bowl of petals and starting to chop them.

"And I shall cut the roots," Azalea said, taking them and cutting them into small pieces.

"Mom," Daisy said, "as it is a day off from school, can Azalea and I go for a long walk around Clover?"

"I think you can," their mother said, smiling. "After you eat your breakfast, of course."

Daisy and Azalea looked at each other and smiled. A nice journey was waiting for them after breakfast.

Daisy and Azalea were very excited while having breakfast with their mother and father, who had joined them.

"Mom, dad, we can't wait to see Clover!" Azalea said. "I think today it is going to be very beautiful, as it is its birthday!"

"Yes, it is very beautiful, my girls," their father said. "I saw it in the early morning. After you go to see the city I and your mommy will also go to have a nice walk, shall we, Marigold?"

"It is a wonderful idea, Marjoram," she said.

"That is great! Azalea and I will go after breakfast," Daisy said. "We will take a long walk," she added, looking at Azalea who was smiling excitedly.

The sisters finished their breakfast hurriedly and swam to their bedroom again, to get ready.

"We shall take our bags, as well," Daisy said, brushing her hair in front of the mirror. She put a pretty golden headband on her head, matching it with her top.

"Yes, you are right," Azalea agreed, opening the closet. They each grabbed their bags and swam out of the house.

"I am so excited, Azalea," Daisy said. "I can't wait to see Beyondness again."

"Yes, me, too," Azalea said. "Let the adventures begin!"

Chapter 2

The Birthday of the City

Clover was very beautiful on that day. Mostly it was a beautiful city every day, but as it was its birthday on that day, it was more beautiful than ever. Bright shells were floating all around the city, lighting it with colorful sparkles, casting rainbow's colors all around. Nightingales of the ocean were singing in every corner, filling the surroundings with sweet melodies. The pretty and colorful city was decorated with luxurious plants and flowers, and it was full of happy mermaids, who were out to celebrate the city's birthday.

"This is amazing," Daisy said, looking around, as they neared the city's gates.

"Daisy, what was the book about what you read yesterday?" Azalea asked. "I know it was about Beyondness, but exactly what was described in that book?"

"The beach," Daisy said. "People were having fun on the beach. I wish we could see it."

"Sounds interesting," Azalea said.

Suddenly Daisy stopped swimming.

"What is it?" Azalea asked, also stopping.

"Azalea, what if we swim at the beach today?" Daisy asked, her eyes sparkling with excitement.

Azalea raised her eyebrows and did not say anything.

"Come on, Azalea!" Daisy said. "I want to see the beach! Don't you want to see it, too?"

"Well, of course, I do!" Azalea said. "But it will take longer than what we had planned. Besides, I don't understand how we shall do all that."

"Look, Azalea," Daisy said, "we can go to the Three Thorn Reefs and get some Pink Sparkle from there. Then we can swim until we reach a beach."

"What if we don't reach a beach?" Azalea asked. "What if the shore is too far?"

"I think Teacher Arlo will help us," Daisy said. "But he may not be at school today. Hmm, let's think."

The sisters sat down on a bench and started thinking about what to do.

"We need to get a map," Azalea said.

"Let's go back home and look in our Worldology schoolbooks," Daisy suggested.

"I always look through my schoolbooks at the start of the term. There was no map there. Maybe we can ask dad if he has a map."

"But then he will want to know why we need it," Daisy said. "Let's return home when mom and dad go to see the city, and then we can find dad's map."

"Excellent!" Azalea said happily.

The sisters swam back home and saw that their parents were not there. Daisy swam to the desk and opened the drawers.

"I shall look in these drawers," Azalea said, opening the closet.

"I got it!" Daisy shrieked, taking out a big parchment from the drawer. "I knew that daddy had the map of the ocean!"

"Wow! Let's have a look at it!" Azalea said excitedly and came to sit next to Daisy in the shell beside the desk.

They rolled open the parchment and looked at it. They were seeing it for the first time. It was a huge map with everything on it.

"Wow, this is so big," Daisy said. "I do not know where to look."

"Let me see," Azalea said. "This is Clover, here," she added, pointing the place on the map, marked with the name of their city. "We need to see where the nearest seashore is."

The sisters examined the map for a long time. Soon Daisy found a shore that was closest to their city.

"Here it is, Azalea!" She shrieked. "And it is not too far from here."

"That is so wonderful!" Azalea said. The sisters memorized the exact location of the shore and put the parchment back into the drawer.

"Let's go, hurry up!" Daisy said, taking her sister's hand, and swam out of their house again.

"We must go to the Three Thorn Reefs at first, right?" Azalea asked.

"Yes, so that we can get the Pink Sparkle," Daisy said. They knew the way to the Three Thorn Reefs, so they started swimming to the city's gates again, looking very excited.

The farther they swam from the city, the darker and more silent it became. There were occasional fish swimming here and there, and random plants grew.

"We are near the Reefs now," Daisy said when they reached the mountain. "Look for the shells."

The mermaid sisters started to look for the magical shells only they knew about. Their Teacher Arlo thought that they did not exist, as it was a myth, but the sisters had discovered the reality of the magical sparkles that could grow them human feet.

"I found one!" Azalea called, taking a small white shell from under one of the rocks.

"It is so good that only we know about the shells," Daisy said. "Otherwise there would not be left any here anymore."

"We need to find more," Azalea said. "You know, the effect of the sparkles goes away fast."

"Here it is!" Daisy said, getting another shell from under a bushy plant. There were two more under another bush. "Now we have four. I think this is enough."

The sisters divided the shells between them and put them in their small bags.

"And now, let's go!" Daisy said, swimming in the direction of the shore that they had found on their father's map.

"Let the adventures begin!" Azalea added, swimming forward.

Chapter 3

The New Friends

"I hope there will not be sharks or medusas," Azalea said. "We do not have dahlias."

"If a shark comes our way, just throw the magical sparkle in its mouth, like the previous time," Daisy said, giggling. "It will grow feet and will be confused."

Azalea laughed, remembering the poor shark that had grown feet a couple of months ago. "It was a very good trick," she said. "I think that shark remembers the strange feet till now."

"When do you think we will reach the shore?" Daisy asked, looking around. They were not familiar with those places, as they were there first time in their lives.

"I have no idea," Azalea said. "But according to the map, it is not too far, and we can reach there in about an hour if we swim quickly."

"Then let's swim quickly!" Daisy said. "On the count of three, we will throw ourselves forward and see how long we can swim if we do our best."

"One, two, three!" Azalea said.

Both of them sprang forward, shaking their pretty tails as hard as they could, pushing the waters back with their arms, trying to be faster than the other.

The water of the ocean splashed past by them, as the pretty mermaids swam fast, without talking. Soon they reached a solid wall.

"Azalea, I think we have reached the shore!" Daisy said happily.

Azalea nodded, looking excited. "Let's go up and see if we came to the right place."

They swam impatiently upwards. Soon they saw the sunlight that was penetrating through the water. "We are near, Azalea," Daisy said. The two mermaids reached the surface and got out their heads. They looked around and gasped in amazement. On their right side, there was a beach full of people, who were swimming, splashing, playing and having fun on the sands of the beach.

"This looks exactly like the picture I saw in my book!" Daisy exclaimed. "I can't believe it!"

"Let's go and see what we can find there," Azalea said. "But at first, let's eat a few sparkles."

"We must not tell anyone that we are mermaids," Daisy said. "People may get scared."

"You are right," Azalea said, taking a handful of sparkles and putting them in her mouth. Daisy did the same.

As they swam closer to the shore, they started to feel how their tails turned into beautiful feet, with pretty turquoise skirts over them.

"I have forgotten how to walk," Azalea said, laughing, as they stood up and started walking towards the beach sands. "I look a bit awkward when I walk like this," she added. Daisy looked at her and burst out laughing. Azalea looked like a raccoon that was trying to model on a podium.

The beach was full of different people: men and women, young boys and girls, children and babies. Some were playing with balls, some were lying on towels, and others were parasailing, while motorboats went in circles near the beach, making the excited people fly in the air. Daisy and Azalea walked on the beach sand, looking around in amazement. Palm trees were decorating the beach, as well as beautiful bungalows and small buildings. There were flowers growing everywhere, and there was a small park nearby.

"This is wonderful," Azalea said. "Unbelievable."

"Just like it was described in my book," Daisy said.

"Hello, girls," a voice was heard behind them.

The mermaid sisters turned around. Two girls of about ten years old were standing behind them with a ball and smiling.

"Oh, hello," Azalea said.

"Hello," Daisy said.

"Who are you?" One of the girls said. "I am Sophia, and this is my friend Anna," she added.

"I am Daisy, and this is my sister Azalea," Daisy said.

"You have such beautiful names!" Anna exclaimed. "Do you want to play with us? Our friends are not here today, and we need more people to play, so we thought you would want to join us today."

Daisy and Azalea looked at each other and smiled, nodding.

"Of course!" They said. "We would love to play with you!"

The girls were rather pretty. Sophia had black hair reached her shoulders, and her black eyes were smiling. Anna's hair was curly and brown, and she had pretty brown eyes. Both of them were wearing colorful t-shirts and jeans shorts.

The girls and the sisters walked to a lesser crowded place to play with the ball.

"I have seen a picture of a ball in my book about Beyondness," Azalea whispered to Daisy as they started to play.

"Let's play volleyball," Sophia suggested.

Daisy and Azalea had a hard time playing volleyball. The ball kept slipping out of their hands all the time, and they couldn't throw it over the net.

"Hey, don't you know the game?" Anna asked. "Where are you from, anyway?"

"We are... we live not far from here," Daisy said. "And you?"

"Our houses are very near to the beach," Sophia said. "We come here to play every day. We have not seen you before."

"Yes, it is because we came to this place for the first time," Azalea said, and Daisy nudged her. "I mean, we only moved to this place yesterday."

"Ah, I see," Anna said. "What games do you like to play? Do you like to play tag?"

"Tag? What is that?" Azalea asked.

"Yes, I think I know," Daisy said, looking at Azalea meaningfully. "You run and chase the others to catch them, remember? We saw the picture..."

"What picture?" Anna asked. "It is a very common game. How come you do not know it?"

"Of course, we know it!" Azalea said at once. "We saw a picture of our friends playing it once, and it was very … um… funny."

Anna shrugged. "All right, then, let's play that game."

Daisy looked at Azalea with excited eyes. She was impatient to start playing. She had seen the pictures of the games that the children used to play in Beyondness. They used to play that game in Clover, as well, with their mermaid friends, only instead of running, they swam. Azalea was looking at her, but she seemed a bit confused. Daisy did not understand what the matter was. Only when they started playing, she realized that Azalea was having trouble running. She was falling and getting caught all the time.

"Azalea, what is going on with you?" Anna asked. "You fall all the time."

"I know," Azalea said, getting up. "It is just… my knee hurt for a second," she said immediately.

"Really? Well, we can go and take a rest for some time," Sophia said. They led the way towards their towels that were on the sand. Daisy and Azalea walked behind them.

Chapter 4

Playing Games

"Daisy, I think it's time to eat some sparkles," Azalea whispered. "The effect will be gone soon, and everybody will notice that we have tails!"

"Yes, you are right," Daisy said, slipping her hand into her bag and getting some sparkles from the shell. She put the sparkles into her mouth quickly, so that no one would notice. Azalea did the same.

"Girls, do you want to take some rest on the towels? We have more towels – it will be enough for the four of us," Anna asked, turning around, just as Azalea closed her mouth full of sparkles.

"Mm-hmm," she said, nodding vigorously.

"Wait, are you eating something?" Sophia asked, looking at Azalea suspiciously.

"Mm-hmm," she said, shaking her head and trying to swallow the sparkles as fast as possible. Some of the sparkles were still on her lips, as she did not have time to wipe her mouth clean.

"Hey, your saliva sparkles!" Anna exclaimed. "That is strange."

"Really? No, it must have seemed to you," Azalea said, hurriedly wiping her mouth. "I think it was the sand. I fell on the sand a few times, and some of it got on my lips."

"Well, maybe," Anna said, as the four girls lay down on the towels, enjoying the sun.

"And what other games do you like to play?" Sophia asked.

"Well, um, for example, fish-racing," Daisy said.

"Fish-racing? What kind of a game is it?" Anna asked, sitting up.

"You swim in the water, and try to be faster than the fish," Daisy said.

"We can't swim," Anna said. "How can you swim faster than fish?"

Daisy and Azalea exchanged glances and smiled. "It is easy," Azalea said. "But if you can't swim, then we can't play that game."

"Hey, I have an idea," Sophia said. "Let's play hide-and-seek."

Azalea remembered that game from her book. She looked at Daisy, who was nodding happily.

"I will count to ten and then start to look for you, all right?" Anna said, getting up at once.

Daisy, Azalea, and Sophia agreed. They started to find a place to hide, as Anna closed her eyes and started slowly counting to ten.

Sophia was soon out of sight. Azalea tried to run, but it was a bit difficult for her to run. She saw Daisy running away. Azalea looked around, thinking where she could hide. As she could not think of a hiding place, she went to the ocean and hid underwater. She raised her head from time to time to see if Anna had started looking for them yet.

"There is Sophia!" Azalea heard Anna's voice. She stuck her head out of the water to see them, and at that moment Anna saw her. Azalea hid underwater again, but it was too late.

"There is Azalea!" Anna shrieked. Azalea had to come out of the water.

"Azalea, how did you hide underwater?" Sophia asked, looking surprised. "You had to breathe, didn't you?"

"Well, it was easy," Azalea said. "I know how to swim, and I got above the water from time to time."

"That is cool," Anna said. "And now I have to find Daisy. Hmm, where is she?"

Azalea looked around, too, but Daisy was nowhere in sight.

"She has hidden very well," Sophia said. "We will come and look for her with you."

Azalea, Anna, and Sophia went to look for Daisy. Azalea was very proud of her sister who had managed to hide so well, that they could not find her.

"I looked behind all the trees around here, and she is not there," Anna said. "I wonder where she is."

"Let's look in the bungalows," Sophia suggested. The girls walked towards the bungalows and searched there for Daisy.

"Azalea, if you were Daisy, where would you hide?" Sophia asked.

"Under the towels," Azalea said. "Let's have a look under those towels," She suggested.

Anna and Sophia looked at her in surprise.

"Why would you hide under the towels?" Anna asked.

"I do not know," she said. "But let's have a look, anyway."

There were towels on the sand, the owners of which were swimming either swimming or playing or simply having a walk along the seashore. The three girls went towards the people's towels that were on the sands. Anna started looking under the towels, while Sophia was standing at the side and giggling. Azalea also chuckled.

"Girls, she is not here, as well!" Anna exclaimed, after looking under the last towel. "Where else can we look?"

"Let's look in the toilets!" Sophia said. Anna ran towards the stalls, giggling. Azalea and Sophia followed her.

"Oh, what is this?" Azalea asked, sounding horrified, as she saw the toilets.

"A toilet… why?" Anna said.

"They look ... strange," Azalea stammered. Anna and Sophia looked at each other and shrugged. Then Anna walked to the showers and looked behind the walls. Daisy was there as well.

"Azalea," Anna said. "Your sister is gone. She is nowhere here. Maybe you should call your parents and let them find her?"

"I think that will be right," Sophia agreed. "Because we can't find her. I am getting worried."

Azalea looked at the girls, getting worried herself. Where could her sister be? They had looked everywhere around the place, and Daisy was nowhere.

"Daisy! Daisy! Get out of your hiding place!" She started screaming, looking around. "We are not playing anymore, and we are getting worried!"

"Yes, Daisy, get out!" Anna and Sophia called together.

"Maybe we should call our parents?" Anna suggested.

"No, it will be better if Azalea calls her parents," Sophia said. "You said you lived nearby, didn't you?"

"Oh, girls, I do not know," Azalea said. She could imagine the looks on her parents' faces if she swam back to Clover and told them that Daisy got lost in Beyondness. "I wish we could find Daisy!"

Anna shrugged, turning to look around again. She shifted her eyes upward in exasperation and frowned.

"Girls? Look over there! Daisy's flying!"

Chapter 5

Flying Mermaids

Azalea looked up into the air at once. Among the parasailing people, there was Daisy, parasailing happily, as her motorboat zoomed around in the water. Azalea shrieked from terror, seeing her sister high in the air. She did not know what to do and started crying.

"Azalea, what has happened? Why are you crying?" Anna asked, who was rather cheerful again, now that they had found Daisy.

"I think she is crying from happiness," Sophia said. "At last we found her."

"No, I am super scared!" Azalea said, cleaning her tears. "How will she get back down? She is so high up in the sky!"

"Oh, she is just parasailing! There is nothing scary there!" Anna said. "I am surprised that you are surprised, Azalea. It seems to me that you do not know anything."

"I know everything about this world!" Azalea said. "But I could never imagine that she would..."

"This world? You speak strange things, Azalea," Anna said. "What do you mean by saying this world?"

"I mean... this place!" Azalea said, getting even more confused. "I am just confused to see her in the air, and that is all."

"Anna, Azalea is scared," Sophia said. "When her sister comes down, then she will relax... ah, here she comes!"

Daisy was coming, looking happy and excited.

"Daisy!" Azalea called, walking towards her.

"Azalea! You will not believe it!" Daisy ran forward, screaming happily. "It was so exciting! Even better than in the pictures!"

"Daisy, you scared me so much!" Azalea said. "I did not know where you were!"

"I was hiding, when suddenly I saw the parasailing sign, which said it was for free today!" Daisy said. "I decided to parasail a bit. I could not hold back," she added, giggling.

"And we had decided that Azalea would have to inform your parents," Sophia said. "We were also getting worried."

"Inform our parents?" Daisy asked, raising her eyebrows. "Oh, thank goodness, you did not inform them. It was not a good idea."

"Wasn't it scary there, in the sky?" Azalea asked.

"Not at all," Daisy said. "You can also try, girls. Let's go!"

The girls looked at each other and nodded. Azalea raised her eyebrows. She did not have time to respond, as Daisy and the girls took her hands and dragged her forward, towards the parasailing center.

"Two of us will be together, and two of you together, all right?" Daisy said, speaking like a professional. "Now those people will attach the tows of the motorboats, and we shall start flying!"

The mermaid sisters were attached to one motorboat by a tow, and the other two girls were attached to another motorboat. On the signal of the guard, the two motorboats started gaining speed, making the four friends rise into the air.

Azalea looked down and saw that the ocean was beneath her feet. As they rose higher and higher in the air, she started screaming with excitement. Flying in the air was the most incredible feeling in the world. Daisy was also shrieking and laughing at the same time. Azalea felt the cool air blowing on her face, as a few seagulls flew past her as if being surprised that she could fly, almost like them.

"Daisy, this is so wonderful!" Azalea managed to shout. She turned and looked at Anna and Sophia that were parasailing next to them, a bit far from them, but still in a short distance.

"I like this!" Anna shouted to the mermaid sisters. Suddenly Anna's facial expression changed. She looked horrified. She nudged Sophia, and both of them stared at Daisy and Azalea with scared faces, pointing at them with their fingers and screaming.

"Are they crazy? What are they doing?" Azalea said, looking at the girls with a confused face.

"Oh, no, Azalea!" Suddenly Daisy shrieked. "Our tails! They have grown back!"

Azalea could not believe her ears. She looked down and saw her and Daisy's long tails dangling below them. They had been so excited in the air that they had not noticed that the tails had grown back. Anna and Sophia were panicking. They were screaming and shaking, staring at the mermaids' tails.

"They are really frightened, Azalea," Daisy said. "Two real mermaids are flying in the air, can you imagine? Look at their faces! Oh, no, they will fall now!"

And she was right. The girls were shaking so much, that the tow loosened and the girls fell into the ocean, rather far from the shore.

"Oh, no, Azalea, look, they fell into the ocean!" Daisy exclaimed. "And they can't swim!"

"What should we do, Daisy?" Azalea said, looking down. "We must jump down and rescue them!"

Daisy started loosening their tow. "Help me, Azalea! Let's loosen this tow and jump into the water."

The two sisters worked on the tow and finally managed to loosen it in a matter of seconds. They fell straight into the ocean from the height. Their tails made it easy for them to swim fast and to find the girls, who were struggling to stay on the surface of the water. Daisy grabbed Anna, and Azalea grabbed Sophia, and they started to swim towards the shore. The two girls were too confused to speak, so they were mostly silent on the way to the shore.

The second they reached the shore, Anna and Sophia turned to look at the mermaids' tails with surprised and scared faces.

"We should have told you about this earlier," Daisy said, looking at the girls with an apologetic smile. The mermaids were lying on the beach sand.

"Yes, we are mermaids, really," Azalea added. "We had magically got feet by the magical sparkles," she got out the shell of the pink sparkles from her bag and showed it to the girls.

"Because we wanted to see the beach and to play with you," Daisy added. "But we did not want to tell you the truth about us because we were afraid to confuse you."

"Apparently now we confused you even more," Azalea said. "Okay, just look," she added, as she and Daisy each took a handful of sparkles and ate them. In a few seconds, their tails turned into two feet, covered with short, pretty turquoise skirts, as Anna and Sophia shrieked again.

"I can't believe this is real!" At last, Anna spoke. "I can't believe I have met real mermaids."

"And become friends with them!" Sophia added. "If you told us before, we would be only happy."

"Well, it is good that you told us at last," Anna said. "If you returned home without telling us the truth, we would never know that we had been friends with mermaids!"

"So you are not upset?" Azalea asked.

"Of course, not!" Anna and Sophia exclaimed in unison.

Daisy and Azalea looked at each other, giggling joyfully.

Chapter 6

New Leaf and a Walk in the City

"So, you only know about our world in books?" Sophia asked as they started walking along the shore.

"Yes! And we wanted to see it so much!" Daisy said.

"I could feel that something was not just right," Anna said. "The way you were talking about everything, the way you were playing, the way Azalea was afraid to call her parents. I definitely could sense that she was weird."

"Yes, and I did not know what to say when you were asking me difficult questions," Azalea said, giggling.

"That is why you freaked out when you saw your sister parasailing, right?" Sophia said. "Now I can imagine how scared you must have been."

Daisy laughed. "Girls, but I like your world so much."

"Oh, but you have not seen our world entirely," Sophia said. "You have seen only a small part of it."

"Yes, Sophia is right," Anna said. "Our world is much bigger and more interesting than just the beach and the games."

"Well, we know several more things about your world," Daisy said. "We have books about your world, which we often read. We call your world Beyondness."

Anna and Sophia giggled.

"You know, what? I think we can show you more of our world. What do you think, Anna?" Sophia said.

"Excellent idea!" Anna said. "We live near the city center, and our city is not big so that we can go for a walk right now."

Daisy and Azalea looked at each other. Both of them were very excited about the upcoming walk in the city. Everything was even better than they had expected in the beginning.

"We shall be very careful not to forget the sparkles," Daisy said. "And we are eager to see your city!"

The four of them started walking towards the city center. The sidewalk was lined with beautiful palm trees, nicely shaped bushes, and plants, as well as green grass. There were benches here and there, with lots of people sitting on them, relaxing. There was a beautiful statue and a fountain in the middle of the park. The statue looked like a mermaid, who was holding a bucket of water, and the fountain was starting from the bucket and falling back into the bucket. It was very interesting to the mermaid sisters, so they stood and watched the fountain for a long time. They turned and looked at each person very closely, too curious about what they were wearing or how they looked.

"What is called the interesting blue pants that nearly everyone wears?" Azalea asked.

"A pair of jeans?" Anna asked. "Do you like it?"

"Totally. But I can't imagine wearing it," Azalea said, shaking her head. "I think they are not comfortable."

"They are comfortable when you have feet, and not a tail," Sophia said, chuckling. "But I like your skirts more than pairs of jeans, by the way. I would like to have such cute skirts."

They reached the city center and looked around. It was a big square, which was rather crowded and noisy.

"Girls, now please stay together, so that no one will get lost," Sophia said. "If one of you gets lost, it will be awful."

"Daisy, please don't go trying to do new things all by yourself, okay?" Azalea said. "I do not want you to get lost a second time."

"Okay, I promise," Daisy said, holding Azalea's hand, to prove that she was telling the truth.

"What is your city called? Ours is called Clover," Azalea asked.

"It is called New Leaf," Sophia said. "This is the Main Square, from which many streets are starting. These are cars and buses, do you see them?"

Daisy and Azalea looked at the streets. Many vehicles were moving rather fast, while people walked on the sidewalks.

"I remember seeing the bus in my book," Daisy exclaimed.

"And I remember seeing the picture of the metro, which goes under the street," Azalea said, looking at the ground, trying to see the metro. "But where is it? How do you get to the metro?"

"There is a special entrance," Anna said, smiling. "Do not worry about it. We can take the metro and go to the zoo later, but now we can walk in the city."

Daisy and Azalea got very excited when they heard about the zoo. In their books, they had seen the pictures of nearly every animal and could not imagine that someday they would see those animals for real.

There were brightly lit shops and cafes in the city, and the mermaid sisters stopped to look at them every few seconds. They could not take their eyes off the colorful things.

"Our Clover is beautiful, too, but your New Leaf is more brightly lit," Azalea said. "Maybe it is because our city's only lights are the floating seashells, and your city is lit with different bright things."

"I wish to see your city someday, but I know it is just a dream because I can't breathe underwater," Anna said. "So, we shall show you around our city. At least you will get to see ours."

Anna and Sophia took the mermaid sisters to look at the city further. When they were crossing the street, Azalea stood in the middle of the street to examine an approaching car. Sophia looked around and saw that only the three of them were safely on the sidewalk. One of them was missing. And it was Azalea.

Sophia turned around just in time to see the approaching car and Azalea who was watching the car in fascination. The car honked a few times, but Azalea did not move. She just stood there, smiling.

"No, Azalea, you can't stand in the middle of the street!" Sophia screamed and ran into the street to get to Azalea. She grabbed Azalea's hands and dragged her towards the sidewalk. Fortunately, Azalea was not harmed by the car.

Sophia was breathless when they reached the sidewalk.

"Are you crazy, Azalea?" She said. Anna was also very frightened.

"No, why?" Azalea asked, not realizing their fear.

"Haven't you read in your books that it is very dangerous to stand in the middle of the street?" Sophia asked. "The street is for cars. When someone stands on the street, she may easily get harmed by being hit by a car. And then it will be very sad."

"I think I have read something about it in one of my books," Daisy said, scratching her head.

"I only wanted to see a car from a short distance, to touch it and to see what it feels like," Azalea said.

"Azalea, you can examine a car in the parking lot, if you want to," Anna said. "When the car is not moving, only then it is safe to get close to it."

"It seems like a shark to me, from what you tell me about cars," Azalea said, laughing.

"I think it is a shark in our world," Sophia agreed.

Chapter 7

The Tastiest Thing in the World

The girls walked in the Main Square, enjoying the beautiful scenery of the city, the metallic statues, the joyful people and the nice sunny weather. There were colorful flowers nearly everywhere, and everything was covered in bright green grass. No wonder that the city was called New Leaf. Daisy and Azalea loved the statues and stopped to examine them every time they saw one. The statues seemed to be real people, only motionless and hard. Daisy loved the flowers, too, while Azalea admired the pretty forms of the bushes carefully arranged on the edge of the sidewalks.

"So, here is an ice-cream parlor," Anna said happily, getting closer. "I have some money so that we can eat ice-cream here."

Daisy and Azalea jumped up and down, shrieking happily. It was because they knew it was something really tasty, as it was described in their books about

Beyondness. They had always wanted to taste it because the books told them it was the sweetest and tastiest thing in Beyondness.

"I can't believe we will eat ice-cream," Daisy said.

"We eat it every day!" Sophia said, giggling, and Anna nodded in agreement.

"You are so lucky!" Azalea exclaimed, as they went and sat down at one of the empty tables.

"We can choose now," Anna said. "Here are the pictures, you can choose any you like, and the waitress will bring it."

"We do not know anything about the flavors," Daisy said. "You choose instead of us. We want the tastiest ones."

"My most favorite ice-cream is chocolate ice-cream," Anna said.

"And mine is vanilla ice-cream with cherry syrup," Sophia said, closing her eyes dreamily. "I can already feel the taste."

"Wow, both sound very yummy," Daisy said. "But I think I will take the chocolate ice-cream, as it sounds better to me."

"And I want to try the vanilla ice-cream with cherry syrup," Azalea said. "And I can't wait to taste it!"

The waitress brought the ice-creams. Daisy took hers and licked it. The second her tongue touched the ice-cream, she shrieked and looked at the ice-cream with surprised eyes.

Anna and Sophia started giggling.

"What happened, Daisy?" Azalea asked with wide-open eyes, who still hadn't tasted her ice-cream.

"It was… it was awfully cold! It was freezing! It was like the special waters of Antarctica that are described in our book of Worldology," Daisy said.

"Really?" Azalea said, sounding suspicious. "Let me try it," she added, sticking out her tongue carefully and touching her ice-cream with it.

"See?" Daisy said, seeing Azalea's eyes opening even wider. Anna and Sophia were still giggling.

"But it is really tasty," Azalea said, as she continued eating her ice-cream.

"You were prepared for the cold, that's why you did not shriek like me," Daisy said, chuckling, as she indulged in her ice-cream like the rest of them.

For a few minutes, no one was talking. They were enjoying their ice-creams, which indeed was the tastiest thing in the world.

"Girls, it was something that I will remember all my life," Daisy said. "I will never forget the taste of this unbelievable thing that you eat every day."

"I wish I could take some home with me and eat a little every day," Azalea said. "By the way, can I?"

She asked, her eyes suddenly opening wider with hopes.

"I am afraid; you can't," Sophia said. "Ice-cream melts very quickly, and it will be gone the moment you swim in the water."

"Oh, I understand," Azalea said. "Well, in that case, I will try to never forget the taste of the ice-cream."

"Girls, there are other tasty things in our world, too, besides ice-cream," Anna said. "For example, caramel, marmalade, cakes, chocolate, cookies and many other things. I think we can try all of them while you are here."

"Really?" Daisy and Azalea shrieked together. The prospect of them eating all the delicious sweets of New Leaf was more than exciting, and it made them happy.

"By the way, how long can you stay here?" Sophia asked.

"We must return home by evening," Azalea said. "Otherwise our parents may worry."

"Oh, too bad that you are not staying at night," Anna said. "We could go to my house, and my mother would make soft beds for you in my bedroom."

"Well, we are enjoying our daytime with you as well," Daisy said. "And we are so happy that we met you today on the beach."

"Girls, I suggest to make the most of our day together and visit the zoo," Sophia suggested. "It is very interesting there, and it is not far from here. We can go walking, or we can take the metro."

"Let's take the metro!" Daisy and Azalea shouted. "We want to see the metro, as well."

Chapter 8

Up and Down, Down and Up

The girls and the mermaids walked to the metro entrance. Daisy and Azalea were very impatient to see the 'train,' as they called it. On the way to the metro, they ate more sparkles, so that not to grow tails in front of people.

"Are the sparkles tasty?" Anna asked, looking at the sisters eating them.

"They have no particular taste," Daisy said.

They reached the escalators and stepped onto them. Daisy and Azalea stayed behind, standing on the ground.

"Daisy, Azalea, just step onto it!" Sophia called, seeing that they did not get onto the escalator with them. But it was too late – they could not get back up the escalator, as it was moving down rather fast and many people were getting on it by each second.

Soon Anna and Sophia disappeared from view.

"Daisy, what are we going to do?" Azalea asked.

"Well, maybe try and get onto the stairs," she said, walking a bit closer and watching it move. She looked attentively just how people were stepping onto it. "Azalea, I think we must put one foot on them and lift the other one up until we feel safe to put it down," she added. "And all the time hold onto the sidebar."

"On the count of three," Azalea said. "One, two, three!" And the sisters stepped onto the escalator. It was not scary at all, now that they were on it already.

"Wow, this is so much fun!" Daisy said, looking around in amazement. "I wonder where Anna and Sophia are."

Another escalator was going upwards, which was right beside their escalator. There were many people on it as well, getting out of the underground. Suddenly two girls waved from the crowd that was going upwards and started shrieking their names.

Daisy and Azalea looked at them, surprised that other people also knew their names, but then their surprise became bigger when they noticed that they were Anna and Sophia, who were probably going back up to help them step onto the escalator.

All four of them were giggling, as the girls went further up, and the mermaids further down, getting separated again.

"Poor girls," Azalea said, as they were nearing the bottom. "They will have to get down now again."

"Careful, Azalea," Daisy said, who was rather strained to see how other people were getting off the staircase. Seeing that they almost jumped when they reached the last step, she held Azalea's hand and waited. "When we get to the last stair, just make a little jump, okay?"

"Okay," Azalea said, getting ready. When they reached the bottom, both of them jumped, landing on the ground safely.

"Wow! that was something!" Azalea said.

"Yes, we have never jumped in my life, but we did not fail," Daisy said. "We seem very comfortable with these feet, I guess," she added.

"Our first jump and so successful!" Azalea said, turning back and seeing Anna and Sophia on the first escalator again. The girls were giggling again, obviously because of their need to go back and forth between the two escalators. When they reached the bottom again and got off, they came to join the mermaids.

"We also had an adventure," Anna said. "It looked as if we could not get enough of the escalators!"

Daisy and Azalea giggled. "It was not so difficult, as it turned out," Daisy said. "And we enjoyed the ride so much!"

"Wait until you get in the 'train,'" Sophia said, smiling. "You will enjoy the ride more."

The ride was really enjoyable for the sisters. They were surprised by the entire moving thing that was carrying them and many other people and children.

"We are almost there," Anna said. "We shall get off at the next station."

"Do your parents let you travel in the city alone?" Daisy asked.

"Of course! Why not? Our city is very safe, and no one gets lost," Anna said. "Whenever someone gets lost, she calls her parents, and they come to get her. Can't you go for a walk in your city without parents?"

"Of course, we can," Azalea said. "Our city is also very safe. And if someone gets lost in Clover, they send the messenger fish to notify their parents."

"Messenger fish?" Anna asked, sounding surprised.

"Yes, the messenger fish know everyone in the city and give or take messages," Daisy said. "So it is not a problem to send a message by one of those fish.

There are many of those fish in Clover, so it is not difficult to find one, too."

Anna and Sophia were amazed by the details about Clover. They wished they also had messenger fish or even messenger birds to give or take messages.

It was time for them to get out. This time Daisy and Azalea did not fall behind when the girls stepped onto the escalator. They followed them as if they had used the escalators their whole lives.

"Are we going to the zoo now?" Daisy asked impatiently. "I can't wait to see the animals! I know nearly all the animals of Beyondness," she added proudly.

"Yes, and me, too," Azalea added. "One of my most favorite books is exactly about the animals of Beyondness."

The mermaid sisters were excited to see the animals. They had seen them only in pictures in their books. When they walked through the gates of the zoo, Daisy barely held her shrieks of happiness, mainly because Anna had told them not to be too noisy, because the animals might get frightened.

Chapter 9

Dolphins Are Amazing Creatures

The zoo was big and beautifully decorated. Each animal had a big area to enjoy nature. The girls saw lions and tigers, bears and wolves, as well as an elephant and a giraffe. Daisy could not go away from the panther's cage, thinking that it was the most beautiful animal in the world, while Azalea decided that the monkeys were the funniest creatures in the world and stood watching them for a long time.

"You can feed the monkeys and see how they react," Anna said, giving Azalea a small bag of fruits that was allowed to give to certain animals.

Azalea took small pieces of apples and threw them through the cage bars, where the monkey caught them and ate them with big noise. Azalea giggled, seeing how the monkey wanted more and was screaming at her for more apples. Daisy joined her, and they started feeding the monkeys together.

"That smallest one is my favorite," Azalea said, trying to toss the apple right to that small monkey baby, which was so fast and flexible that it snatched the apples even from the other's hands.

"It is so cute!" Daisy exclaimed. "It looks at you, Azalea. It probably wants more."

Azalea could stay there forever, but the girls told them that it was getting late and they still had other animals to see. The zoo was rather big, and there were still many things to see there.

"You know, there is a big dolphinarium here," Anna said. "They have great shows."

"Oh? A dolphinarium?" Daisy exclaimed. "We learn Dolphinian at our school! I can speak the language of dolphins!"

"Yes, and me, too!" Azalea added. "Daisy, we can communicate with the dolphins!"

Anna and Sophia were rather impressed.

"That sounds interesting," Sophia said. "We can hear while you talk with them. I am so impatient!"

Soon they reached the dolphinarium. The dolphins were in the water, splashing around happily. The worker told the children that there would be no show at that time, because the trainer had lost her whistle, and her dolphins reacted only to the sound of that whistle. There was no other whistle exactly like that one, so the show was postponed.

"Oh, it is so sad," Anna said, turning around. "Come on, girls, we can't see the show today."

"That is too bad," Sophia said. "I wanted you to watch the show, Daisy, and Azalea." The girls turned around and saw that Daisy and Azalea were standing close to the edge of the dolphins' pool, communicating with the dolphins.

"Oh, Anna, they are communicating! Listen to them!" Sophia exclaimed. The mermaid girls were emitting strange squeaking sounds, just like the sounds the

Dolphins made. Sometimes it seemed to Anna that the sisters were only pretending to be speaking with the dolphins because the sounds were rather funny.

"Anna, Sophia," Azalea said excitedly, "the dolphins told us that the trainer's whistle is deep down in the water, lying on the ground. It is very thin and small, and they can't pick it up with their mouths. They do not know how to let them know."

"Are you serious?" Anna exclaimed. "I will go and tell the guards right now so that they will retrieve the whistle."

"No, no, Anna, do not tell them," Daisy said. "They will not be able to get the whistle – it is too deep on the floor of the pool. But we can do it!"

"Really? What about your feet?" Sophia asked.

"Swimming with feet is more difficult, but we can breathe underwater, so it is not a problem at all," Azalea said. "Come on, Daisy, let's go! We will be able to see the dolphin show today!"

Anna and Sophia watched in amazement as the two mermaid sisters jumped into the pool. Just at that moment, the guards came running and shouting.

"Stop the girls! You can't get in! The pool is very deep! Get out right now, or we will get you out."

"Do not worry, sirs, the girls can swim very well," Anna said. "They decided to get the whistle for the trainer, so that the show would take place, anyway."

"But how do they know where the whistle it?" One of the guards asked.

"Well, they think it is on the bottom of the pool," Sophia said, looking at Anna and smiling. "Let's hope they are right."

Before the guards could say anything else, Daisy and Azalea appeared on the surface again, accompanies by the dolphins. Daisy was holding the whistle. The sisters' eyes were glowing with happiness.

"Hey, that is the whistle!" The guards exclaimed when the sisters got out of the pool and gave the guards the whistle. "How did you know that it was in the pool?"

"The dolphins told us," Azalea said, and Daisy giggled. The guards thought the girls were joking, so they also laughed.

"All right, so the show will take place, thank you very much for retrieving the whistle," one of the guards said.

"But I still do not understand, how can you swim so well?" The other guard asked, scratching his head.

Daisy and Azalea shrugged and giggled. They went to sit in the front row, to watch the show. Gradually the hall started to get filled with people, who were hoping to see a good show.

"The dolphins told us that they love to do the show and to make people happy," Daisy said. "They told us that they enjoyed these shows no less than the people."

"And what else did they say? Did they say anything about us?" Anna asked.

"Yes, they said that you and Sophia were very beautiful," Azalea said.

"Oh, they did?" Sophia exclaimed. "I will wave to them now so that they will know that I know what they said about me."

Daisy and Azalea also waved to the dolphins, joining Anna and Sophia. The Dolphins did a back-flip together, and it seemed to Sophia that they were smiling.

Chapter 10

Goodbye

The dolphin show was interesting and fun. After the show, the girls decided that they were hungry.

"What do you want to taste now? We have already eaten ice-cream, but there are many other tasty sweets, as well," Anna said.

"I would like to eat marmalade this time," Daisy said.

"And I want a cookie," Azalea said.

Anna suggested that they get what they want from the nearby store and continue walking in the city. There were many different sweets shops all around the city, and it was not difficult for the girls to find one. Daisy decided to try cherry marmalade, and Azalea wanted a chocolate chip cookie. Anna and Sophia chose chocolate bars, and the four of them started eating the sweets.

"Is there anything sweet in Clover?" Anna asked, eating her chocolate.

"Yes, of course!" Daisy said. "For example, we have the Thornless Cactus, the Blue Juice, the Ribs of Petals and some more."

"Thornless Cactus?" Anna repeated, her eyes open wide. "That is something I would like to try."

"The Ribs of Petals also sound interesting to me," Sophia added.

"But none of them even come close to the ice-cream," Azalea said. "Even though they were my favorite before I ate ice-cream today, but now I am sure none of them is as good as the ice-cream."

"Yes, they are also tasty, like this marmalade, for example," Daisy said. "But the ice-cream is the number one for me."

"And for me, too," Azalea said.

Anna and Sophia nodded, smiling.

"We also like ice-cream like nothing else," they said. "We could ice-cream for breakfast, for dinner, and for supper!"

"And for lunch, too," Daisy added, giggling.

When they finished eating, they noticed that it was almost evening. It was time for the sisters to go home. Otherwise, it would get dark, and their parents would worry a lot. Daisy and Azalea decided to return to the beach, but the girls did not want to let them go without getting them a souvenir.

"There is a small shop right around the corner," Anna said. "I think I know what we can give you to take home." She got two hair-clips. One of them looked like the flower daisy, and the other looked like the flower Azalea.

"Wow, exactly like our names! Thank you so much!" Daisy exclaimed, taking her hair clip and attaching it to her hair. It looked pretty.

"Yes, I think you will always put this on your hair and remember us by them," Anna said.

Azalea put her flower clip onto her hair. "I will always have this in my hair," she said. "Thank you very much!"

"We also have something to give to you," Daisy said, getting the empty shell of the pink sparkle out of her bag and giving it to Sophia. "Azalea, you give yours to Anna, so that they will also have something to remember us by."

"Thank you!" Anna and Sophia said, smiling. "These are treasured gifts for us."

"I think it is time for us to go," Daisy said, looking up at the sky. "Let's walk to the beach together. Then we shall go into the water, and you will go home."

The girls agreed. Daisy and Azalea ate the last of the pink sparkles, and the four of them started walking to the beach. There were still lots of people on the beach, still playing and relaxing.

"We live near the beach," Anna said. "So we are almost home."

"We will miss you and all the adventures we had in your wonderful city New Leaf," Azalea said. "I will remember everything for a very long time."

"Girls, you can come up anytime you want," Sophia said. "We are almost always on the beach when we are not doing homework, of course," she added giggling. "But we shall continue our friendship, which is very special to me."

"I will always keep this beautiful clip in my hair and remember you," Daisy said. They had already reached the shore.

"And we shall keep these wonderful shells and remember you," Anna said. "Have a nice trip!" She added, as the mermaid sisters waved and walked into the water.

*****

"Daisy, I can't believe we had another wonderful adventure," Azalea said. "I can't even decide, which one was a bigger and better adventure – the time when we rescued the prince or this one?"

"I also can't decide," Daisy said. "But my idea at night was a really good one."

"Have such great ideas often, my dear sister," Azalea said. "Due to you, today we had one of the best days in our lives."

The sisters swam the rest of the way as fast as they could because Clover was far and it was getting dark. The sisters did not want their parents to worry about them.

Clover was still brightly lit, and everyone was celebrating. As the sisters reached the city, their tails grew right back again. They were eager to swim at their house and discuss their adventures in the bedroom.

Their mother and father were at home, relaxing.

"Hi, mom, dad," the sisters said, entering the house.

"Hi, girls," their parents said. "Did you have a good time?"

"We had the best time in our lives," Daisy and Azalea said together. They looked at each other and smiled meaningfully.

THE END

Conclusion

Diana Molly is a writer for children who enjoy writing as much as reading. Her books mainly focus on friendship, efforts and good lessons. She believes that children learn from books, and any good book is like a good friend that can give only good advice. The number one reader of her stories is her own daughter, who enjoys her mother's stories and always waits for more to come.

Diana Molly likes the story of Paper Bag Princess and believes that girls can be adventurous and strong, instead of being weak and fearful. The young readers can see this reflected in her stories, where the girls are the main heroes and solve problems better than many boys could have done.

Printed in Great Britain
by Amazon

59531972R00050